EGMONT

We bring stories to life

First published in Great Britain in 2006 by Dean,
an imprint of Egmont UK Limited,
239 Kensington High Street, London W8 6SA

Thomas the Tank Engine & Friends

A BRITT ALLCROFT COMPANY PRODUCTION

Based on The Railway Series by The Rev W Awdry

Photographs © Gullane (Thomas) Limited 2006

© Gullane (Thomas) LLC 2006

ISBN 978 0 6035 6232 7
ISBN 0 6035 6232 9
1 3 5 7 9 10 8 6 4 2
Printed in Singapore.

No Sleep for Cranky

The Thomas TV Series

DEAN

Brendam Docks was always very busy. Cargo ships came there from all over the world.

Poor Cranky the Crane, who worked at the Docks, was never allowed a nap. He worked all the time – day and night. So he was always cranky.

One morning, Cranky was unloading some pipes from a cargo ship and putting them into trucks.

"Ahoy there, Cranky!" called Salty, the Dockyard Diesel.

"Where have you been?" snapped Cranky.

"Well, that's not a very cheerful way to say 'hello'," Salty replied.

Next, the twin engines Bill and Ben arrived for work. "Hurry up, you two!" shouted Cranky. "I haven't got all day."

"You're no fun," grumbled Bill.

"You wouldn't be fun if you were stuck up here by yourself," snapped Cranky.

"So that's why you're so cranky," said Ben. "You're lonely!"

"I am not," Cranky cranked.

"If you're lonely, I'll keep you company," said Salty.
"I could tell you a story."

Salty loved nothing better than to tell stories about the sea. But everyone else thought they were boring!
"Not another one of your stories!" groaned Cranky.
And he carried on lifting pipes.

"I was in the middle of a wild storm…" began Salty.

But Cranky didn't want to listen.
He was so cross that he dropped the pipes all over the track!

The pipes rolled towards a big shed.

CRASH!! They hit it so hard that the shed came tumbling down! Bill, Ben and Salty were trapped.

"Whoops," said Cranky, quietly.

"You're going to be in big trouble," giggled Bill and Ben.

The Fat Controller was in his office, being measured for a new waistcoat. When he heard the news, he went straight to the Docks.

There was a big mess. The Fat Controller needed Harvey the Crane Engine to clear it up. But Harvey was on the other side of the island and wouldn't get there until the next day.

The Fat Controller had to speak to Cranky through a megaphone. "You have made a terrible mess, Cranky," he called, crossly.

"I'm sorry, Sir," whispered Cranky.

"Bill, Ben and Salty," said The Fat Controller. "You will have to stay here until Harvey can clear up this mess in the morning."

"This reminds me of a story," began Salty.

"Not another one of your stories," groaned Cranky.

Salty spent all night telling Cranky about wild storms, dangerous adventures and brave ships. Cranky tried not to listen. But he couldn't get away!

When the sun rose, Salty was still talking. "I can't take any more!" creaked Cranky.

At last, Harvey pulled up. "I'm here to clear away this mess!" puffed Harvey.

Cranky was so pleased that he forgot to be cranky. After all, once the mess was cleared up, Salty and his stories would go away.

"I'll never be cranky again," promised Cranky, after Salty left. "As long as I don't have to listen to any more of Salty's stories!"

Cranky worked hard all day. He carefully loaded the trucks. He even said 'please' and 'thank you' to the engines.

"Cranky is being very polite!" puffed Thomas to Percy.

"I hope it will last!" smiled Percy.

But as time went by, Cranky went back to his old ways. He became crankier than ever.

"Oh well, it was nice while it lasted," said Percy to Thomas.

"Yes," said Thomas. "And if Cranky gets too cross, we know what to do."

"What?" asked Percy.

"We'll ask Salty to tell him a few more stories!" smiled Thomas.

The engines laughed, but Cranky didn't think it was very funny!